FRANCES DEAN

Who Loved to Dance
and Dance

.TO ALL THOSE WHO LiVE
WiTH ALL THEiR HEART

First published 2014 by Walker Books Ltd
87 Vauxhall Walk, London SE11 5HJ

2 4 6 8 10 9 7 5 3 1

© 2014 Birgitta Sif

The right of Birgitta Sif to be identified as author/illustrator of this work
has been asserted by her in accordance with the Copyright,
Designs and Patents Act 1988

This book has been typeset in Aunt Mildred

Printed in China

British Library Cataloguing in Publication Data:
a catalogue record for this book is available from the British Library

ISBN 978-1-4063-3798-3

www.walker.co.uk

FRANCES DEAN

Who Loved to Dance and Dance

BIRGITTA SIF

WALKER BOOKS
AND SUBSIDIARIES
LONDON · BOSTON · SYDNEY · AUCKLAND

Once there was a girl,
whose name was Frances Dean.
She loved to dance and dance.

At school sometimes, while no one watched,
she danced with her fingers on her desk.
Or gently she tapped her toes to the beat
of her teacher's voice.

But mostly she couldn't wait to go
outside and dance!

When no one was around,
she would feel the wind
and dance ...

and hear the singing of the birds
and dance and dance and dance.

But when people came about,
all she could feel were their
eyes on her ...

and she forgot how to dance.

Then one day
the birds

who always loved
her dancing

showed her something
unusual.

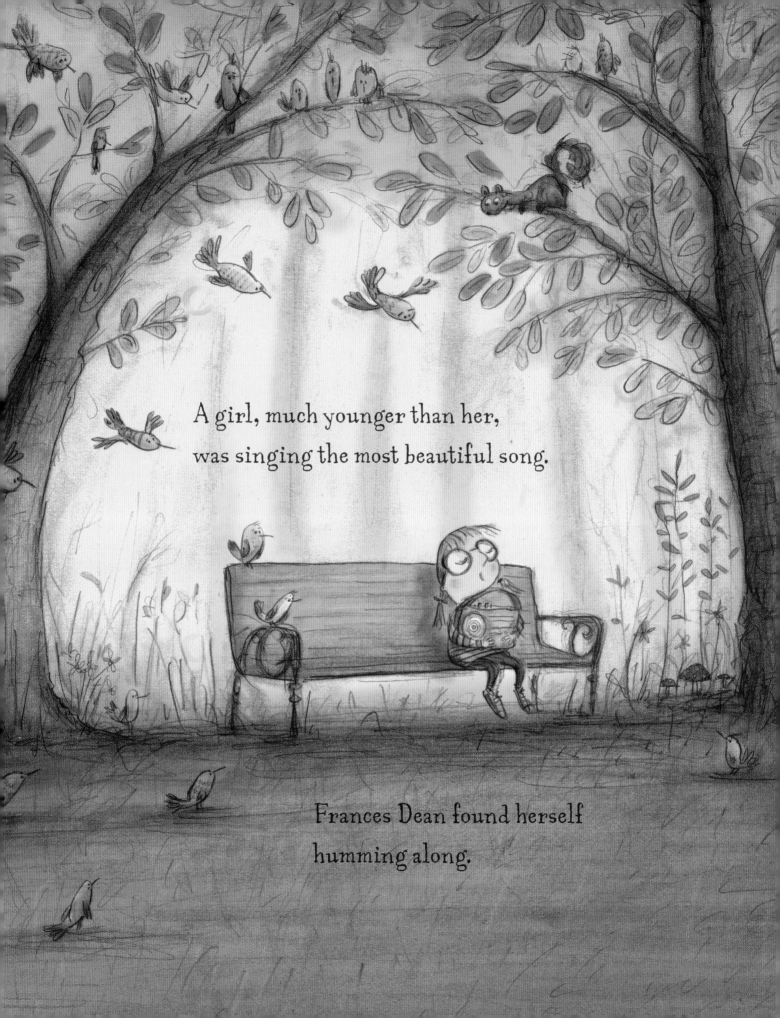

A girl, much younger than her,
was singing the most beautiful song.

Frances Dean found herself
humming along.

That night Frances Dean couldn't sleep.
She couldn't stop thinking about the
little girl and how she had shared her
beautiful song.

Frances Dean wondered if she would
ever be able to share her dance moves
like that.

The next morning when she woke,
Frances Dean felt the wind and heard
the singing of the birds.

And she was reminded with all her heart
how much she loved to dance and dance.

So while no one was around
she practised her dance moves.

And when she was ready
she let the wind move her.

And shyly she asked the birds,

"Can I show you my dance?"

She asked her cat, "Do you know how to dance like this?"

She even did a jig with the neighbour's dog.

And when she met the old lady in the square,
she showed her how to twist.

Later on, the little girl,
with the beautiful song,
asked Frances Dean,
"Can you show me how
to dance, too?"

And she did.

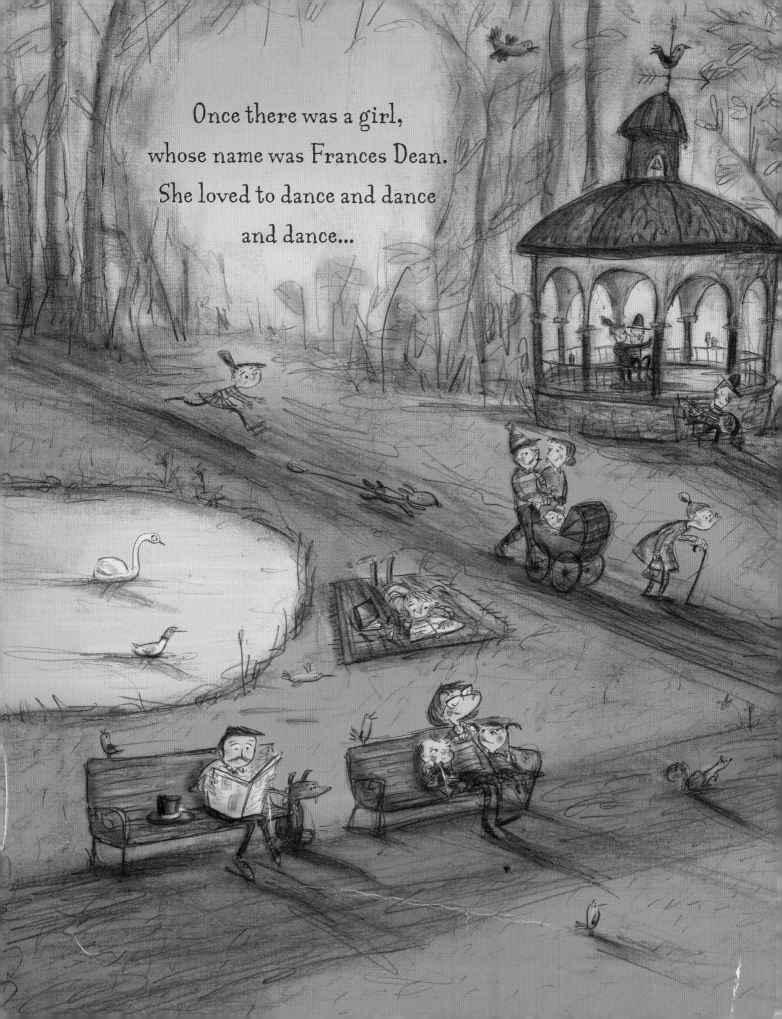

Once there was a girl,
whose name was Frances Dean.
She loved to dance and dance
and dance...